Kareem and the Time Machine

Inventor: Garrett Morgan Volume 2

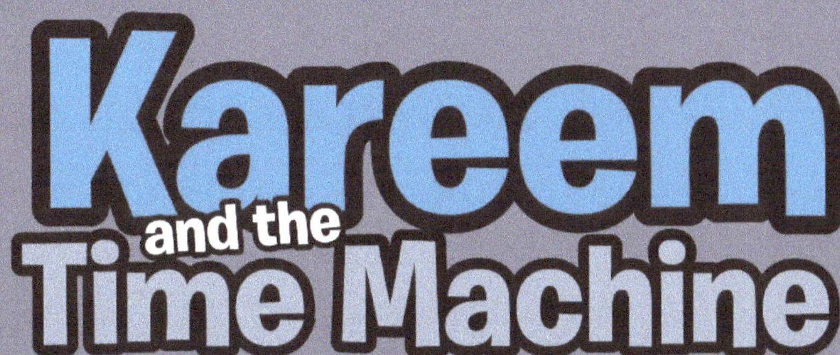

Lonnie Thomas

Published in the United States of America
ISBN 978-1-962730-10-5 (SC)
ISBN 978-1-962730-12-9 (HC)
ISBN 978-1-962730-11-2 (Ebook)

Lonnie Thomas
222 West 6th Street
Suite 400, San Pedro, CA, 90731
www.stellarliterary.com

Ordering Information and Rights Permission:

Quantity sales. Special discounts might be available on quantity purchases by corporations, associations, and others. For details, contact the publisher at the address above.

For Book Rights Adaptation and other Rights Permission. Call us at toll-free 1-888-945-8513 or send us an email at tlonnie14@yahoo.com

This week black history lesson is on:
Mr. Garrett Morgan
1891

The teacher said, "Today's African American children lesson is on Mr. Garrett Morgan. Mr. Morgan was born in Kentucky in 1877. This period in history 1865–1876 was known as the Reconstruction period. The Emancipation Proclamation, made in 1863, was meant to end all slavery. But slavery did not stop in America until after the Civil War, which ended in 1865. Texas was the only state to hold out, but it did so a month later. Mr. Morgan's parents were ex-slaves throughout this period, which gave them the right to vote, hold public office, and own land (1865–1876)."

REST ROOMS
WHITE
BLACK

"The 1876 election ended this experiment for Reconstruction and instituted a new form of government for African Americans called Jim Crow laws. These laws took away their right to vote, run for public office, or use public water fountains unless they were marked for colored people. These laws went into effect in all the Southern states. Mr. Morgan ran away in 1891 at the age of fourteen, leaving behind ten brothers and sisters. He moved to Cleveland, Ohio, and began work in a sewing machine factory."

At this moment, Kareem began to think of what life must have been like for a boy of fourteen. Kareem set the date to 1891 on his time machine.

1891
5

Boy, I wonder what it must have been like in a big city
without your family in those days, Kareem thought.

"Hi, Garrett, what are you doing?" asked Kareem.

"Working on my bicycle so I can go to work," said Garrett.

"Why do you have to work?" asked Kareem.

"Because my family are sharecroppers back in Kentucky. They live off credit until the crops come in, then pay their bill to the store, and buy more seed for the next growing season. There's never enough money left over, so I send back money to help the family," said Garrett. "I'm happy to be able to send back money for my ten brothers and sisters."

"What's your name?" asked Garrett.

"Kareem."

"Well, Kareem, my name is Garrett Morgan, and I have to go to work. Nice meeting you, Kareem," said Garrett.

Kareem set the time for when Mr. Morgan was a man working in his lab.

"Hello, are you Mr. Garrett Morgan?" asked Kareem.

"Yes, I am," said Mr. Morgan.

"My name is Kareem, and I would like to ask you a few questions if I could, if you have the time," said Kareem.

"Yes, I do. Go right ahead, young man," said Mr. Morgan.

"What was it like growing up and working away from your family?"

"Well, in 1891, there were no child labor laws. Kids worked ten to sixteen hours like the adults. I worked at a sewing machine shop where I studied, worked, and observed sewing machines. I invented a new sewing machine and belt fastener. In 1907, I opened up a sewing machine repair shop. "

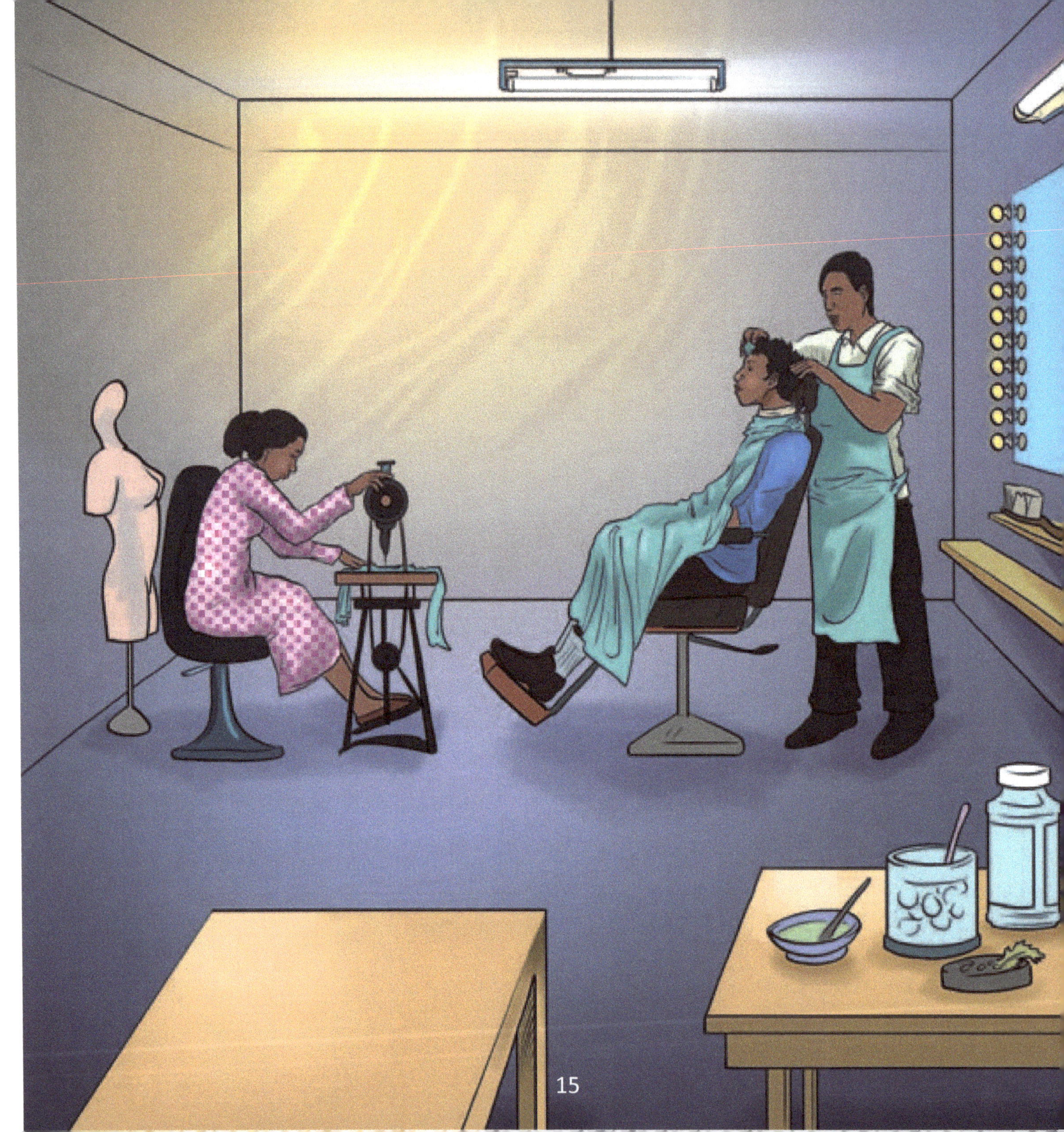

"In 1908, I married Mary Anne at the age of twenty-one. We opened up a tailor shop, and I created a cream that straightened the hair. This product made me wealthy. In 1916, when America entered the war to save Europe, I invented a gas mask, and my brother and I tested it by going into a tunnel. An explosion had happened under Lake Erie. We saved two men's lives. "

"This gas mask was used in World War I by American soldiers. Chemical warfare was used in this war, and gas drifted in the air. Soldiers and townspeople were killed by the thousands. A treaty was signed after the war to not use chemical weapons in other wars by all nations. The gas mask today is used by firefighters. "

TRAFFIC SIGNAL

"In 1920, because of the widespread use of cars, auto accidents began to make street safety a problem. I invented the traffic signal, which later became the traffic light."

Cleveland
Call

"I later created a newspaper called the Cleveland Call and gave money to our great black college."

"So you can see, Kareem, you don't have to create something entirely new. It only has to be an improvement or a new way to use a product. All inventions should help life be more enjoyable or improve human condition. One of the keys to invent something is to learn to observe. You will begin to see a lot of things that can be improved upon."

"Kareem, Kareem, did you finish your black history homework?" asked his mother.

"Yes, Mom, I did," said Kareem.

"Because if you did, you can go outside and play with your friends," said his mother.

"Mr. Morgan, nice meeting you. That's my mother. I have to go. Goodbye, Mr. Morgan."

TRAFFIC SIGNAL

"Simon says, 'STOP!' Simon said, 'GO!'"

"Wow! I wonder if that's how Mr. Morgan first came up with the idea for the traffic signal."

If we can see something, that is not right, not fair, not just. You have a moral obligation to do something. You can not effort to be quiet or to be silent.

We must not be silent.

Congressman John Lewis
January - 2217

I'm talking about voting rights. The reason that we are the only country among advanced democracies that makes it harder to vote is it traces directly back to Jim Crow and the legacy of slavery. And it became sort of acceptable to restrict the franchise. And that's not who we are. That shouldn't be who we are. That's not when America works best

PRESIDENT OBAMA gave this respond as part of a question on voting rights. Question asked by April Ryan a black journalist. Jan. 18 2017

DEDICATION

Micheal Lee Tiller, Xachi Anthony Pope, Jordan Mitchell, and Emmanuel Montgomery, I hope that all your dreams of what you want to be in life come true. These are some that are freely given. Son, Brother, Father, and Elderly Stateman. Always remember that your greatest treasure is in your family and friends. Because by observing, listening and asking questions. They can teach you what wrong, right is, and help you achieve your dreams, and all young man that would be of age, to my two grandsons, Aaron T. White and Rashakill Thomas. I love you all.